Original Korean text by Sang-wu Shim
Illustrations by Hye-ryeon Jang
Korean edition © Yeowon Media Co., Ltd.

This English edition published by Big & Small in 2015
by arrangement with Yeowon Media Co., Ltd.
English text edited by Joy Cowley
English edition © Big & Small 2015

ISBN: 978-1-921790-85-0

Printed in Korea

The Happy Prince

A story by Oscar Wilde
retold by Joy Cowley
Illustrated by Hye-ryeon Jang

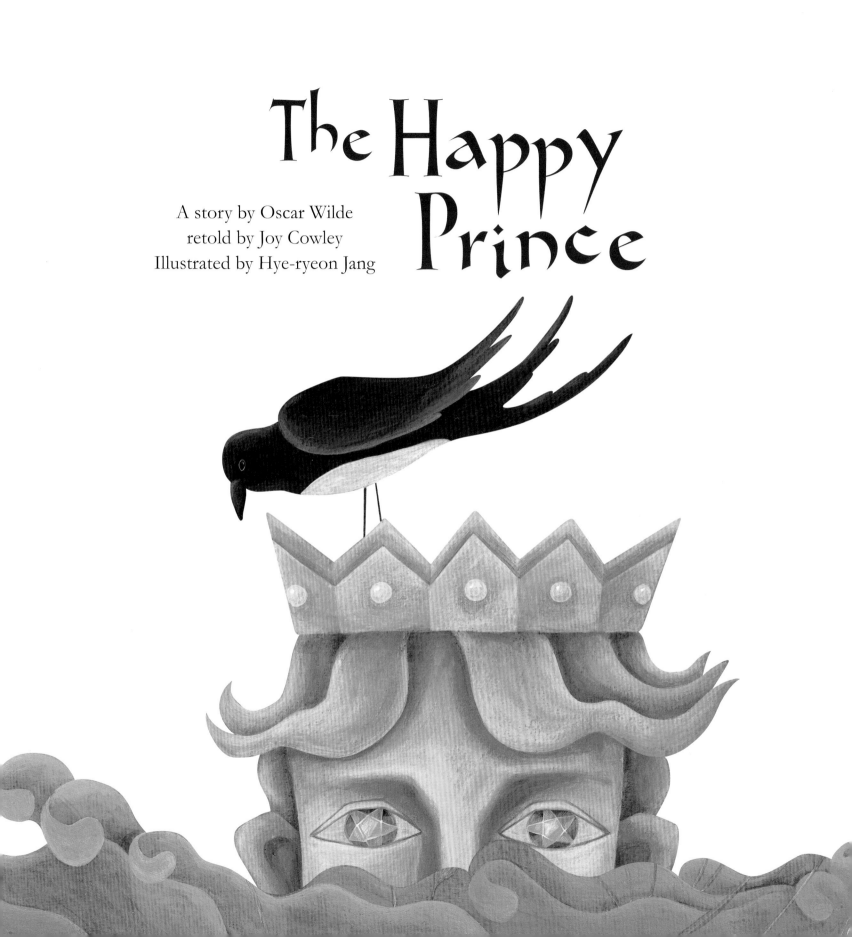

In the middle of a city
stood a statue of the Happy Prince.
The statue was covered in pure gold.
His eyes were blue sapphires.
There was a red ruby on his sword.

Everyone admired the prince.
"We are lucky to have this statue."
"What a beautiful prince!"
"He looks like an angel!"

One day, a swallow came to the city.
When night fell, it looked for shelter
and it saw the statue of the Happy Prince.
"I will sleep here tonight," it said.

The swallow slept between the feet
of the prince, but was awakened
by falling drops of water.
The swallow looked up and saw
that the Happy Prince was weeping.

"Please tell me why you are weeping," said the swallow.

The prince said, "Everyone calls me the Happy Prince,
but I see many sad things in this city."

The prince went on,
"In a narrow alley lives a poor woman.
She is very tired and her son is sick.
He has a high fever, but she has no money
to buy the medicine that would cure her son.
Little swallow, will you do something for me?
Take the ruby from my sword
and give it to that poor woman."

With the ruby held in its beak,
the swallow flew to the woman's house
and dropped the ruby on the table.

The woman cried, "What a miracle!
Who has brought us this ruby?
I can now buy some medicine for my son."

The next day, the swallow said,
"Happy Prince, I must leave you.
Winter is coming and my friends
have already left for warmer lands."

"Little swallow, stay one more day," said the prince.
"In an attic, a young man is writing a novel.
He has had no food for days.
He is nearly fainting from hunger.
Take the sapphire from one of my eyes
and give it to that young man."

The swallow did not want
to pluck out the sapphire eye,
but it did as the prince asked
and took the sapphire to the attic.

The young man was so overjoyed
that he wept with gratitude.

The next day, the swallow said,
"It is getting colder. I really must go."

"Swallow, my friend, just one more day,"
begged the Happy Prince. "Please!
The match girl in the city square
has dropped her matches in the sewer.
Her father will be very angry
when she gets home.
Will you take the sapphire from my other eye
and give it to the little match girl?"

"You will not be able to see!" cried the swallow.

"That does not matter," said the Happy Prince.
"I will be all right. Please do this for me."

The swallow took the other sapphire eye
and dropped it into the hand
of the little match girl, who cried,
"Oh! What a pretty gem this is!
It must be worth a lot of money."

The swallow flew back to the prince.
"Now you can't see anything.
I will stay here and be your eyes," it said.

"No, little swallow," said the Happy Prince.
"Go to the warm land before it is too late."

But the little bird refused and again
slept between the prince's feet.

The next day, the prince said to the swallow, "Fly around the city. Tell me what you see."

The swallow flew from street to street. When it came back, it told the prince about all the poor people it had seen.

The prince said, "My body is covered with sheets of pure gold. Take it. Give it to all those poor people."

Bit by bit, the swallow took the gold off the prince's body and gave it to the poor.

Winter came and snow started falling.
Being cold and tired, the swallow could not fly.
It kissed the feet of the prince.
"Goodbye, my prince," it said and then died.

The next day, the city's mayor said,
"What has happened to our statue?
The Happy Prince has changed to a beggar.
Take the statue down and throw it away!"

The swallow was thrown on a rubbish heap
and the prince was dumped on a fire.
But the fire could not melt the heart
of the Happy Prince, and his heart
was thrown on the rubbish heap
beside the dead swallow.

God asked one of his angels
to find the two most precious things
in the world.

The angel came back with the swallow
and the heart of the Happy Prince.
They were both reborn as angels
and remained friends forever.